The Queen Cat

Written and Illustrated
by
BETSY WARREN

Steck-Vaughn Company
An **Intext** *Publisher*
Austin, Texas

Library of Congress Cataloging
in Publication Data
Warren, Betsy.
    The Queen Cat.
    SUMMARY: Pam describes the activities of
her special Queen Cat which seem similar to
those of ordinary cats.
    [1. Cats—Stories]   I. Title
PZ7.W2498Qe   [E]   72-176070
ISBN 0-8114-7742-8

ISBN 0-8114-7742-8

Library of Congress Catalog Card Number 72-176070
Copyright © 1972 by Steck-Vaughn Company, Austin, Texas
All Rights Reserved. Printed and Bound in the United States of America

I am Pam.
I have a cat who thinks
she is a queen.

Every morning I run
to look out my window,
and there she is—
          the QUEEN CAT!
She always wears a coat
of white fur, and it shines
like snow in the sun.
She sits high on her
throne and keeps her eyes
shut.

When I run out the back
door, the Queen Cat opens
one eye.

"Good-morning, Your Royal
Highness," I say. "Will
you have your breakfast now?"

The Queen Cat stands up.
She yawns. She stretches.
    Then she leads the way,
and I follow. No one EVER
walks in front of royalty,
you know!

"Your Highness, here is your milk," I say.

She laps it with her little pink tongue.

Princesses and queens do like milk VERY much, you know!

When she finishes her
breakfast, she washes
behind her left ear,
then behind her right ear.
Members of royalty ALWAYS
wash behind their ears,
you know!

"And now, Your Royal Highness," I say, "what would you like to wear today?"

First she tries on a dress with dots on it. I help her put it on.

She is not sure that she likes it.

Then she tries on a
green velvet dress with
a soft, red sweater.
I button the sweater
for her.
    She LIKES it.

Then she puts on fuzzy
slippers and a little bonnet.
Last of all she puts on
her jewels. I help her.
You know that royal ladies
always wear LOTS of jewels.

When the Queen Cat is
dressed, she sits on a
cushion while I read
her favorite stories to
her.
　She closes her eyes so
that she can listen better.

The book reads: the LITTLE RED MOUSE

After the stories, I bring
paper and pencils to the
Queen Cat. She writes
while I hold the pencil.
I can read my name—
PAM.

When the Queen Cat
wakes up from her nap,
I say, "Your Royal
Highness, it is time to
take your afternoon ride
in the sunshine."
    Royal ladies do LIKE to
go for rides, you know!

The Queen Cat also likes to climb trees. No matter how loud I cry, she won't come down.

Members of royalty only climb down out of trees when they want to!

But when I say, "Your Highness, here is your supper of fish," she comes down out of the tree.

Even princesses and queens get hungry, you know!

After she eats her supper
and washes herself again,
she goes to sit by the fire
to watch TV.
Her favorite programs
are the same as mine.
We watch together.

31

After that I say,
"Good-night, Your Royal Highness."
She goes to bed, and . . .

so do I.